ISBN 0-86163-481-0

Copyright © 1989 Award Publications Limited

This edition first published 1990
Second impression 1994

Published by Award Publications Limited,
1st Floor, Goodyear House,
52-56 Osnaburgh Street, London NW1 3NS

Printed in Singapore

Tales of Oaktree Wood

VICKY'S NEW HAT

by Rene Cloke

AWARD PUBLICATIONS LIMITED

Vicky, the fox cub, was very excited.

"I have been asked to look after the flower stall at the bazaar tomorrow," she told her friends in Oaktree Wood.

"Money is being collected for the baby animals' holiday-treat."

"What fun!" cried Rusty Rabbit,
"We'll all go to the bazaar."
"We will collect some flowers
for you," said Filbert and
Sally Squirrel.
"Thank you," said Vicky,
"my new hat will be
just right for a flower stall;
I will put it on
and you shall all see it."

Vicky fetched her new hat.
All the animals thought
it was beautiful – but,

– a sharp wind blew it from
Vicky's head and it
floated off over the grass.

"Oh, catch it, catch it!" cried Vicky.
They all chased it but they were
not quick enough; the beautiful hat
blew into the river.

The ducks dragged the hat
out of the river. The wonderful
hat was ruined.
Vicky was very sad.

"I shall have to wear my old hat," she said, "this one is soaked," and she walked off with it dangling from her paw.

"Let's try to make a fine new hat for Vicky," suggested Rusty, "I'll collect some rushes to plait together."

"I'll find some flowers to decorate it," said Filbert.

"And here are some pretty feathers," said
Penny Pigeon.

Flippy Frog helped Rusty to gather some rushes and,
together, they wove them into a bright little
green hat.

The squirrels and Mandy Mouse made a daisy-chain and picked a bunch of forget-me-nots and buttercups to trim the hat. Then they fastened the little feathers at the side.

"I hope it's the right size," said Filbert, "it looks very pretty."

It was and Vicky was delighted.

She started off for the bazaar with two
huge baskets of flowers, one on each arm.
The little hat was perched on her head
and she wore a new blue dress.

"Goodbye!" she cried, "and thank you all
very much."

The others waved goodbye as she
walked through the trees.

"Sell all the flowers!" cried Mandy Mouse.

"And don't let your hat blow
off again!" called Rusty.

The bazaar was held in a little glade in the
middle of the woods.

Vicky arrived in good time to set up her stall.

She put bunches of flowers in bowls and vases
and made buttonholes and garlands for
people who wanted flowers to wear.

Then she decorated the stall with trails of ivy, creeper and pine-cones and set the pot plants on the ground.

Everyone said it looked beautiful and Vicky felt very pleased.

She had time to walk around and look at the other stalls.

There were stalls full of clothes, tea-cosies and egg-cosies and all kinds of pretty things.

Belinda and Billy Bunny had jars of sweets
and boxes of chocolates as well as toffee,
fruit and cakes on their stall.

Some of the toffee had not hardened very well,
so while Billy was wrapping it up in small
bargain packets; quite a lot of it stuck
to his paws!

At three o'clock,
the bazaar was opened by
the famous Miss Gwen Goose
who was well known for her
beautiful paintings of
farmyard scenes.

"I am sure everything will
be sold," she said, "and I would
like to thank you for the lovely
bouquet you have given me,"
and she waved the bunch of
flowers to show that everyone
could begin to sell and buy.

There was much clapping and cheering and Miss Goose bowed and curtsied.

The animals gathered round the stalls; some tried their luck in the bran-tub and some tried guessing the weight of an enormous cake that Billy Bunny pushed around in his wheelbarrow.

There was a tent where tea was served and a stall for ices and fruit drinks.

Then the sports began.

Rusty Rabbit was winning the egg and spoon race easily.

Suddenly he stepped on a piece of the sticky toffee and couldn't run any further but he slipped off his shoe, ran on, and came in first after all.

Some animals said that Flippy Frog shouldn't have been allowed in the sack race because he was too good at hopping. But, since he was the smallest in the race, he was allowed to take the prize.

The three-legged race was the most exciting.
No one seemed to be able to run straight and
just as Sally and Filbert Squirrel were passing
Vicky's stall they lost their balance –
Crash! Over went the stall!
Over went the vases and all the lovely flowers
were broken and scattered on the ground.

Everyone ran to help
the squirrels and the
flowers were trampled on.
    "Oh, dear!" moaned Vicky.
"All my flowers will be
crushed and broken and I won't
have any money to give
to the bazaar."

She tried to pick them up and to collect the vases that were not broken but the excited animals stepped on her paws and at last she gave it up.

She wandered off to a quiet corner and, sitting down by a water-lily pond, she sobbed and sobbed.

No one noticed her for a long time. Vicky was
quite startled when she heard a kind voice cackle -
"Why, what is the matter?
Have you hurt yourself?"

Vicky looked up
and there was the famous
Miss Gwen Goose bending over her,
holding, under one wing,
her bouquet of flowers.

She looked so kind that Vicky told her
all about the flower stall.

"Well, well!" said Miss Goose. "This is a
sad tale, but we'll soon fix everything!"

She held out a wing to Vicky and the
little cub clutched it eagerly.

"Come with me and I'll see what can be done."

They hurried off to the busy glade where
the stalls were set up.

The little rabbits and squirrels
helped to put up the stall again and
cleared away the crushed
flowers. Soon everything
was tidy.

"Now," said Miss Gwen Goose,
"we will arrange my lovely
bouquet into buttonholes and posies
and see if we can sell them all!"

Vicky thought this was
a splendid idea.
They had so many
customers that in ten
minutes every flower was
sold and Vicky's money box
was so full that it
wouldn't even jingle!

And that was not the end of the excitement.
There was a grand parade of the stallholders
and a prize for the prettiest hat.
    "The prize goes to Vicky the fox cub,"
called out the judge and he
presented Vicky with a
big box of chocolates.

"Plenty to share with all those who
have helped me," said Vicky
delightedly.